Crybaby The Legend of La Llorona

Edwin C. De La Rosa

ISBN-10: 1491291664
ISBN-13: 978-1491291665

Preface

La Llorona, or Cry Baby, is a wives tale. There are many tales such as this, but few have endured centuries. I have tried to keep religion and politics out of our tale and stay as true to the legend as possible. I had heard the tale in many forms in the last forty years most of them had three things in common, beauty, a magic potion, and an unspeakable horror. Personally I had always considered La Llorona as a wives tale designed to keep children away from water ways after dark. That was until I decided to write this tale and start my research. To my surprise there were police reports, eyewitness accounts and victims of La Llorona as recent as two-thousand-thirteen. My skepticism meant little to eyewitnesses or victims. The victims that could or would speak offered their blind eyes and white hair as proof of the beauty and the horror they had seen. Whatever they saw, it was real to them. They claimed to have seen a beautiful young woman crying near the water searching for her children, but as they came closer her Medusa like appearance was so horrid it turned their hair white. The lucky ones lost their sight; those less fortunate lost their souls. The exact origin of this legend is unknown. I have heard it in eight languages in sixteen different countries; but some of the oldest versions seem to come from Spain, sometime in the mid-fourteen-hundreds.

This is my personal version of the tragic tale of a young beautiful courtesan, whose willingness to do anything to maintain her beauty, might have trapped her here, till the end of time. La Llorona or as I have named her Cry Baby: Wives Tale, Myth, Legend or tortured soul, judge for yourselves.

CONTENTS

Cover Design by Edwin and Chasity De La Rosa

of Krystal Rose Productions Houston

Photography provided by John Trotter of John Trotter

Photography

Model is Silvia Salamanca from Mallorca, Spain

Skully by Edwin De La Rosa

ACKNOWLEDGMENTS

We would like to thank all of the persons whom have inspired us to continue with our works. Unfortunately naming each of these individuals would take a lifetime. So for the moment please permit us stick to the major characters, while never forgetting even the minor influences in our story. I am your humble host Edwin C. De La Rosa and we thank you for taking interest in our simple tales. I would like to thank God and my brother David Arturo De La Rosa who raised me after my mother's death. Which left me and my next eldest brother Amando orphans at age four and eleven. Thanks to these three the word impossible is not a part of my way of life. I would also like to thank Chasity Johnson soon to be Chasity De La Rosa whom without none of this would be possible.

1 NEW WORLD DISORDER

Houston, Texas, USA 04:30 October 19th, 2018; a small group of police officers are hard at work blocking off a crime scene. Flashing emergency lights and a large swarm of flies accompanies them. Two officers wearing facemasks cover what seems to be a body on the ground as a third officer pukes his guts out, because of the horrid smell.

Their Sergeant is busy trying to take information from an eyewitness to the supposed crime;

“It was La Llorona, I’m telling you!” exclaimed the white haired man. “She did it; she sucked the life out of him. I saw her with my own eyes.”

“Calm down sir,” says Sergeant Ramirez trying to calm the man down “We will take your statement in a minute.”
Sgt. Ramirez redirects his attention to a detective arriving to the crime scene.

“Detective Johnson. what brings out to the river this early?” asks Sgt. Ramirez.

“I heard you had a fresh homicide, thought I’d take a look at it. Does it look as bad as it smells?” says the detective as he covers his mouth and nose with his handkerchief.

"No, it's much worse," says the Sgt. as he uncovers a maggot infested corpse. "It's like he has been here for weeks, but that's impossible with the foot traffic in this area from the local clubs," claims Sgt. Ramirez "It's like someone dumped it here sometime between 2:30 and 4:00 in the morning." "What's really strange is the only footprints near the body; seem to match the victim's shoes."

"Anyone see or hear anything?" asks the detective.

"Yes we have an eyewitness claiming to have seen everything, but there is a slight problem," states Sgt. Ramirez shaking his head.

"Are you kidding? That's great! Where is he?" Exclaims the detective.

"It's the blind guy with the white hair," says Sgt. Ramirez as he points the man out.

"He claims he saw La Llorona suck the life out of our victim with his own eyes."

"Please explain two things sergeant. How does a blind man see anything and what the hell is a la rorona?" the detective asks.

"Well he claims she took his sight after she killed the victim and its pronounced La Llorona (La Yorona)," Sgt. Ramirez tries to explain. "She is a myth or demon from Hispanic Folklore condemned to roam the earth for her crimes." A hazmat team in full Bio-gear arrives along with the Coroner to collect the remains.

The sergeant continues his tale as an early morning thunderstorm begins, "I had not heard her name mentioned since I was a child. The legend says she was a very beautiful young girl in the world's oldest profession." His voice is drowned out by thunder and with a flash of lightning;

We are transported to another time and place.

2 OLD WORLD WIVES TALE

The place is a beautiful green meadow just outside of Cadiz, Spain. The time, mid 1400's near the end of summer as the sun begins to set. A loving Grandmother calls the children away from their play near the river.

"Vamonos ninnios el sol se esta vahando, rapido, rapido oh se los lleva La Llorona!" She proclaims as she rounds the children up to a modest cottage. After dinner the children beg Grandma to tell them the tale of La Llorona.

"Abuella dinos el cuento de La Llorona!"

"Mama why do you tell these tales to the children?" says her daughter.

"So they can learn not to do the same, and for them to stay away from the river at night. Remember your Uncle Tomas was left blind when he saw her. Gather around children I will tell you the tale. La Llorona was a beautiful young girl with a very evil heart."

The grandmother's tale takes us to palace of opulence and ill repute. The palace was a grandiose place with marble columns and gold leafed mirrors. The music and wine flowed endlessly as guests enjoyed themselves feasting and dancing.

Many notorious well to do Pirates, Highwaymen, Dukes, Counts and even future Kings came to enjoy wine, women, song and games of chance. This was indeed a true pleasure palace with some of the most beautiful women from all over the world.

The Crown Jewel of the Palace was Angelica, a flawless beauty, whom always demanded a handsome price for her company. We join her as a Count from France arrives.

The Count's footman removes his cape and dusts his master's clothes off as he exits his carriage and enters the Palace.

"Bonjour mon Cherri; I have brought you a gift," he says as he claps his hands, while the footman kneels holding out a small box. "A small token of my gratitude for the pleasure you bring me," he boasts as he bestows a necklace of blood red rubies around her neck.

Angelica quickly escorts the Count to her private chambers. There she begins her signature dance. With every twist and serpent-like turn another item of her clothing lands upon the floor revealing more of her perfect figure. Every time her silky smooth skin brushes against the Count, her pouting red lips repeat the same question. "How much are you willing to spend on all this?" Angelica pleads. The Count is helpless; he showers her with his entire purse of gold coins. Angelica blissfully rubs her body with the gold as if bathing in it; the Count then greedily devours his prize.

Over the next few months, Angelica was happy collecting her fortune from dignitaries, criminals and even a Sultan. They were all welcome as long as their purses were full. Excitement, splendor and fortunes laid at her feet. Life was perfect for the young courtesan. Then late one evening one of her favorite dresses didn't quite fit.

"It has to fit you must be doing something wrong!" Yells Angelica

"Maybe you have gained weight? My lady," suggest the servant.

"How dare you? My waist is impeccable get out of my sight!" says Angelica tapping the servant on the head with her fan. Another courtesan named Nadia comments on the subject as she enters the room.

"Aye ninia don't be mad; in our business there are many reasons for gaining extra kilos here and there."

"That is ridiculous my diet is very strict," proclaims Angelica.

"Well maybe one of your customers left you a little visitor," Nadia says laughingly as she pats Angelica tummy.

"No! This cannot happen to me! I have been careful to use the honey and herbs!" Angelica exclaims. "I will not have a child ruin my perfect body!" "Nadia what will I do?" "I cannot become fat and ugly!"

"Calm down," Nadia answers. "Some of the other girls say there is a Wizard that lives near the river. They claim that for a small price he can make a potion that will rid you of the child."

"Great let's go see him." Angelica pleads.

"No!" Nadia whispers in a secretive tone. "You must go alone and after dark or he will not see you, for fear of the local priests and what they may do to him for helping you. Look for a shack near the bend of the river directly beneath the moon." Angelica quickly changes into more suitable clothes for travel. Then smoothly talks a young yet eager stable-boy into lending her a horse and buggy. She climbs into the buggy and is quickly on her way as the stable-boy dreams of the promises her body seems to make.

3 PRICE OF BEAUTY

A strange fog grows from the ground as she nears the rivers bend. She searches for the shack fruitlessly, and then remembers Nadia had said it would be directly beneath the moon. So she looks at the moon and as she looks beneath it, a shack seems to grow from the fog.

Angelica slowly stops beside the shack and exits the buggy, cautiously walking towards the door which is open.

"Is anyone home?" she calls.

"Yes," A deep voice answers.

"My na-" Angelica is cut off before she can finish.

"Your name is Angelica, we know, and you have a problem, of this, we are all aware. You've come for my help, but are you willing to pay the price?" The Wizard inquires.

"Yes," she responds "I will pay any price to be rid of this child. I don't want to have a child, it will ruin my life."

"Agreed; then I must gather a few things to make your potion," announces the Wizard as he beacons her into the cottage. Angelica marvels at the size of the inside of the tiny cottage. Its walls were made of stone and the ceiling seemed twenty feet high. There was even an indoor garden and an endless hallway big enough to drive a carriage through.

She is startled as the Wizard commands. "Now sit and give me your hand." He pricks her finger with a needle and collects some of her blood in a white bowl then sets it on a table, covering it with a plate; as he does this Angelica notices his beautiful necklace.

It is a simple gold chain, but it is as thick as a man's finger and the pendant hanging from it is a gold circle surrounding an upside down pentagram with a sixty carat ruby at its center. "What a magnificent necklace," she says. "This old thing? I've had it forever," he answers.

"Good, now for the blood of another

flower." He continues as he limps towards a group of beautiful flowers named poppies and carefully cuts a small incision on several of the pods beneath the blooms. Then carefully gathering their green blood with his index finger and putting it into a black bowl. He then adds water and mixes the contents and pours it into the white bowl mixing once more, while uttering strange words from some long forgotten language. Next he dumps the mixture into a smoldering caldron.

"Well, now for the final item; a small sacrifice from the Earth herself: Mandrake Root. Put this wax in your ears, for if he screams when I pull him from the ground it will leave you quite mad," he informs her.

The Wizard kneels on the ground; as he does Angelica thinks she sees a goat's hoof extending slightly from beneath the wizards cloak she shakes her head and looks again, but now the cloak is covering his feet.

"Here is one," the wizard whispers; as his hands reach towards the dirt it seems that the earth itself tries to avoid his touch. He plunges both hands into the dirt and grasps a root, a root that resembles an infant. The root squirms, clinging to the earth, trying to pull itself back into the dirt; its blood curdling infant like screams are deafening as it loses its grip on his mother earth, his fight is done as life slowly leaves him. "Ah that's better, a quick rinse and in you go," says the wizard as he rinse the root and tosses it into the pot. The root lets out one last lonely cry which seems to echo into the night.

"You shall have your potion soon," the wizard informs her. "But you must follow my directions exactly to the letter. Upon leaving you must drink the entire potion, then go straight to the river, remove your garments and wade into the water. Moments later you will feel a sharp pain but do not worry; it will subside as the river rids you of your unwanted guest."

The wizard fills a vial from the pot with a ladle then carefully corks it and places the vial to cool on a wooden stand.

"Remember do not remove your unwanted visitor from the river," he continues "just leave it behind, for it is no longer your concern; return to your life of leisure and enjoy. Now, here is your potion and hurry while the night is young."

After he rushes her out the door, Angelica realizes the gold she brought as payment for the Wizard is still in her hand. Quickly she turns back towards the cabin, but it is gone. Why it was almost as if the Earth itself had swallowed it. Oh well, she thinks to herself, no harm intended, no crime committed.

The young beauty toasts the moon with her potion and drinks the entire contents of the vial. The potion is smooth and warm yet it causes her to cough as it flows through her. She feels her inhibitions disappear as she continues towards the river, removing her garments with each dance like step of her silky, long legs finally revealing her statuesque body under the light of the moon as she nears the water's edge. Angelica tests the water with her toes and is surprised to find the water warm and inviting. She wades waist deep caressing the surface of the water with her hands. The river responds in kind welcoming her delicately smooth skin with its warmth. Supporting her ample bosoms like a gentle lover she has never known; with only the moon to bear witness of their gentle encounter.

Then suddenly she feels a sharp violent pain entering her body; she reaches towards the shore in vain, but she cannot escape the icy cold grip of the river. Her body thrashes in the blood filled water uncontrollably as she feels her womb being ripped apart. Every nerve in her body seems to be on fire as electricity flows through her veins. When the pain slowly subsides the water seems cold and uncaring as Angelica shamefully walks onto the shore and covers her nakedness. She cries uncontrollably as she searches her very soul for a reason to her sadness. She stumbles back to her buggy and once dressed she returns to the palace, but everything had changed.

She was consumed with loneliness; gold and jewels no longer brought her pleasure. She had changed; no longer seeming to bring men the pleasure they craved. In time she was no longer one in a million, just one of many.

Angelica searched for the Wizard many nights, for months on end. Wandering the rivers banks hopelessly; until one night directly beneath the moon, out of the fog appeared his cabin. She runs to the door and knocks. The door slowly opens and voices in unison from inside beacon her to come in.

"Angelica welcome we have been waiting for you."

" Mi ninio donde esta mi ninio?" (My child where is my child) Angelica asks.

"En el Rio." (In the river) the voices answer. The voices all seem to be coming from the Wizard every time he speaks.

"Please give me back my child." Angelica begs. "I'll pay you anything," she pleads as she pours a fortune of gold and jewels onto the wooden table from a silk bag.

"That is not possible, the child belongs with us in the river," the voices answer.

"But it is my child you must give it back!" she demands.

"No!" the voices answer in anger, as thunder and lightning fill the air. "We warned you there would be a price to pay; and you agreed to pay any price to be rid of the child. Your child will stay with us in the river forever ah ha ha!"

"No no!" Angelica exclaims as she exits the cabin running towards the river in the pouring rain.

She runs into the river in the lightning and thunder crying "Mi Ninio! Mi Ninio!

Donde esta Mi Ninio!" (My Child! My Child! Where is My Child?) "Mi Niño! Mi Niño!" She screams at the top of her lungs as she thrashes the water with her arms. The storm and the river seem to swallow her alive as the thunder slowly roars to a whisper and all is quiet all is dark.

Once again we find ourselves in the living room of modest cottage as Abuellita (Grandma) finishes her tale. "Since then, many people have claimed to have seen a beautiful woman near the river searching for her child. Mi Ninio she cries; but if you get too close you will see her for what she truly is, a creature so hideous that looking at her directly will leave you blind. Worst of all, if she catches you she will suck out your soul trying to replace the soul of the child she lost. Now off to bed before La Llorona gets you." The children quickly obey as they scamper to their rooms emitting childish little "boos" on their way to bed.

4 MORE QUESTIONS THAN ANSWERS

A ringing phone brings us back to modern times and the desk of Detective Johnson.

"Homicide, Johnson speaking; yes, I'm on my way." "Hey Sgt. Ramirez the M. E. just called they got cause of death and ID on your victim. I'm about to go down there, do you want to tag along?"

"I wouldn't miss this for the world," Ramirez replies as he grabs his coat. Both men exit the room as Ramirez dawns his coat. After a short drive they arrive at the morgue. The M. E. is a short, thin, balding, hyperactive male in his mid-forties; he greets them while finishing a slice of pizza as they enter the room.

“Come on in boys care for some pizza?” Johnson and Ramirez quickly shake their heads no.

“So, what was the cause of death Doc?” asked Ramirez.

“He drowned,” replies Doc.

“Just another drunk falling in the river,” adds Johnson.

“Oh no! Certainly not just another drunk, he is Bernard Tumas, CEO of H.G.” interjects Doc “and his blood alcohol level was only a .04; and FYI he did drown but not in that river, the water in his lungs was way too clean and had no traces of chlorine or other chemicals; besides that this man is six two and the river is only three foot in that area." Doc continues as he peels a piece of the shirt off the rotting corpse. "What is really strange is his clothes are mildewed, almost as if it had not been cared for in years; and the corpse itself seems to be decaying at an alarming rate; if I didn't know better I'd say this man has been dead six weeks."

"So what's causing the accelerated decay Doc.?" Johnson asks.

"I've eliminated several bacteria," Doc elaborates, "And found no toxins, so I have come to only one possible conclusion, Time; it is as if the deceased has step though a time warp, where everything happens faster, hours go by in minutes. In other words Mr. Johnson, I don't know."

"Well it looks like we are back to square one Ramirez." says Johnson. "Let's go visit our witness and see what he really knows." both men leave the morgue as the coroner enjoys one more slice of pizza.

5 BLIND MAN'S TRAGEDY

After a couple of traffic jams and a few curse words, Johnson and Ramirez arrive at a hospice. Sgt. Ramirez inquires about their witness at the front desk. "Hello, I am Sgt. Ramirez and this is Detective Johnson, we are here to see a mmmm," Ramirez pauses for a moment while looking at his Smartphone.

"Mr. Johnny Garcia, he was brought in by the paramedics this morning."

"Oh yes the crazy blind man, you

know it took two doses of medication just to get him to calm down and a third dose to put him to sleep. He just kept rattling on about some demon that was out to get him," the attending nurse answers.

"Is he awake now? We need to speed-…" Ramirez is interrupted by a crazed man wielding a metal rod with an I.V. bag still attached to it yelling at the top of his lungs.

"Stay away from me!" Johnny say as he swings in all directions "I can't see you, but I can hear you and you ain't getting me you old bitch!" Ramirez and Johnson quickly tackle him and with the much needed help of two rather large male orderlies manage to restrain Johnny to a straight-jacket and wheelchair then quickly move him out of the hall and into a private room.

Once in the room Ramirez attempts to speak to Johnny.

"Calm down, Johnny, its Sgt. Ramirez, we met this morning. I just want to talk to you, there is no need to be scared,"

"Scared, you think I'm scared?" Johnny answers quickly "Johnny ain't scared of nothing, man or beast."

Johnson interrupts

"Now I know where I've seen you before; you're Johnny Star the world wrestling champ. I saw you defeat the Beast for the title belt just a couple of years ago, what happened?"

"Cocaine happened to me," Johnny states. "Cocaine makes a man do some stupid shit and now this bitch comes along and takes Johnny's eyes!"

"Calm down Johnny we're here to help you," Johnson adds.

"Help me? How you gonna help me?" Johnny rants on. "What did someone do? Turn my eyes into the lost and found or does one of you two just happen to have an extra pair of eyeballs laying around?"

"No Johnny, we're just cops trying to catch a killer," Ramirez affirms. "So help us, tell us what you know about what happened last night near the bayou."

"Look," Johnny calmly proceeds. "I know it sounds crazy but my eyes worked last night. I've been clean for six months and working as a bouncer at Pleasures

Gentlemen's Club. My apartment is just a short walk away. So after a long night, I was on my way home about 2:45 in the morning and I heard what I thought was a woman crying. I hurried my steps because she was crying, mi Niño! Mi Niño! I was sure someone's child had fallen into the bayou. Once I turn the corner I froze in my steps, because just a short distance away was the most beautiful woman I had ever seen. She had long curly hair that was black as midnight down to her tiny little waist, but she was not skinny; oh no! She was sporting double D's and her backside was perfect. I know because she was only covered by a thin veil that revealed her every curve in the full moon's light. Then a man about six foot tall approached her, at first her weeping made me think he had hurt her and she may be in need of help."

"Boy was I wrong; suddenly without warning a deafening roar came out of her mouth accompanied by a green mist. The man was helpless; her sharp claws grabbed him by both arms and forced him to his knees. She opened her mouth wide, almost like a snake does, then her large grotesque worm covered tongue forces its way down the victim's throat as snakes came out of her hair and bit the poor man all over his face. At first I could see the man bleed out of his eyes and nose but then it was like she sucked it all back in and you could see his skeleton under his skin then she tossed his empty carcass to the ground and the maggots covered him up eating what was left. I carefully tried to step back but it was too late, she heard me; as she came towards me I was paralyzed and as her mouth opened wide all I could see was darkness and death. Suddenly I heard gunshots and sirens but I couldn't see so I laid there in the dark until you guys showed up."

"Until this morning; I thought La Llorona was a myth, an old story to scare kids, boy was I wrong."

"Well Johnny thanks for all your help," says Johnson sarcastically.

"We better get going Ramirez before La Rorona gets us."

"Hay I'm not crazy you'll see!" yells

Johnny “She’s real, I’m blind not crazy, you’ll see!”

“What do you make of all that.” Johnson mumbles as they leave the room.

“Well it’s a pretty elaborate tale, how could anyone come up with a story that big in such a short time frame?” Ramirez asks.

“Don’t tell me you believe in all this voodoos, mumbo jumbo?” Johnson retorts.

“All I’m saying is maybe we should check with his employer and find out if it’s true he could see last night, if that’s a lie then the whole story stinks.”

“So you do believe this hocus pocus now I’m blind shi-...” says Johnson, as Ramirez cuts him off.

“I only believe the facts and the facts

are; he knew the victim was six foot and covered in worms. Now how about that trip to Pleasurz? I bet they got cold A/C."

"Ok, but this doesn't mean I believe any of this witchcraft bologna, it just means it is too hot out here to argue." Johnson adds as both men jump in their car and drive off.

6 DETOURS AND DEAD ENDS

Upon arriving at the gentlemen's club, they are met just inside the door, by a large bouncer who informs them to pay the check girl the cover.

"You may pay the girl ten each for cover." the bouncer growls.

"No we're just here to speak to the manager." Ramirez states.

"He is at the bar, now pay the girl or leave," the bouncer reiterates as he blocks their path.

Johnson smiles as he gently pushes Ramirez back with his left arm and says "I got this." The bouncer snidely smiles as Johnson pulls his wallet from his coat pocket, then he realizes his mistake as Johnson flips open his wallet with his I.D. and badge as he comically says, "Oh my God, what do we have here? A fat man that thinks he's funny:" As he pushes the bouncer into the wall he asks him;

"Do you think this is funny, fat man?"

"No sir," he answers.

"Then I suggest you stay out of my way," Johnson explains. "Now who and where's your boss?"

"He's the blonde guy in the blue shirt at the end of the bar," The bouncer answers quickly.

"After you Mr. Ramirez," says Johnson as he releases the bouncer. Ramirez introduces themselves to the club manager as they approach him. "I'm Sgt. Ramirez and this is Detective Johnson we would like to ask you a few questions."

"Sure I've got nothing to hide I am Mafesto, but everybody just calls me Mac," he answers, as he shoos a couple of bikini clad girls away. "Now if this is about Angel not having a license to dance here. I have already explained to vice, she was a new arrival from Vegas. She was supposed to have gone to transfer her dancer's license to Houston. Unfortunately she never came back to work once she paid her tip out and collected her cash out on the cards, she vanished."

"It's a shame because after three months customers are still asking for her and try as they do the other girls just can't seem to replace her."

"No Mac this is not about Angel and we are not Vice. This is about Johnny Garcia and we are with Homicide," says Ramirez.

"I told him not to hit so hard; who did he kill?" Mac asks.

"Nobody," Ramirez confirms.

"Then why isn't he at work? He's two hours late," Mac inquires.

"Whoa Mac, we'll ask the questions here!" Johnson reaffirms. "Now, did Johnny work here last night and how long has he been blind?"

"Yes he did work last night, but blind?" Mac continues, "Johnny isn't blind, why he can see better than most of us even in the dark."

"Well thank you for your cooperation Mac, we'll be in touch if we have anymore questions," Ramirez quickly closes the conversation as he gives Johnson a signal with his head that it's time for them to leave.

The officers converse in the parking lot after exiting the club. "So what did you make of all that?" asks Johnson.

"I always get a little suspicious when someone gives up more information than I asked for Johnson, maybe we should check with Vice about that girl Mac mentioned

Angel," Ramirez suggests.

"You might have a point; missing people and dead people sometimes travel the same road," Johnson adds.

"I do believe he was being honest about Johnny's eye sight, but I don't believe he doesn't know where this girl named Angel is," Ramirez continues. "Who was he trying to convince? We never asked about her or any other girl? Let's go see what Vice knows."

"I still don't believe that Corona crap," says Johnson. As both men jump in the car and head for downtown.

Soon the officers are at the Vice squad office inquiring on the missing girl.

"Hey Captain Harvey, long time no see," say Johnson.

"Well, well, look what we have here? I thought you'd forgot where the basement was since you made detective," answers Harvey.

"Now, how could I ever forget the dungeon, Cap? I did five years here and got to know so many colorful people. This city looks so different from down here; why I bet I met every pusher, pimp and prostitute this city has to offer," says Johnson.

"So what can we do you for," implies Harvey

"We wanted to check up on a missing girl named Angel that was working at Pleasurz about three months ago; got anything on her?"

"Let's see, Pleasurz…Angel… Yup," as he looks at his computer. "But not much, she's not officially a missing person; we tagged her with a warning for dancing without a city license. She is a looker, there's her picture, she had a permit out of Las Vegas but that's no good here. One of our boys ran her I.D. for wants or warrants after they did the follow up, because the manager of the club said she quit. Her real name is Angelica Flores, age nineteen, from McAllen, Texas. She came up clean except that her alleged husband tried to file a missing persons report after she ran away because he wouldn't let her have an abortion."

"Well Ram, looks like another dead end," Johnson grumbles.

"Yeah I guess most of these young dancers just aren't willing to give up that perfect body to become a mom, but that doesn't exactly tie her into a murder case," Ramirez agrees.

"Okay Captain Harvey thanks for all the help but we better keep moving before this case goes cold," says Johnson.

"No problem Mr. Big time detective don't be a stranger you're welcome in the dungeon anytime," Harvey affirms. "You too Ramirez. Mi casa, es su casa" he adds.

"Sure thing, Cap." Ramirez agrees.

Both officers return back upstairs to homicide division somewhat baffled by all the dead ends this case seems to generate.

7 THE QUEST

"You know Ramirez I don't believe in this voodoo legend but maybe our murderer does," Johnson states.

"What do you mean by maybe the murderer does?" Ramirez asks.

"Maybe our murderer is using this legend as a blueprint to commit murder," Johnson continues. "Maybe it's all smoke and mirrors and maybe he is using a legend to cover his tracks, maybe he's using a mythical monster to keep us from seeing the truth."

"You mean kind of like that zodiac killer from years back?" Ramirez asks.

"I mean exactly like that zodiac killer except this guy is using La Llorona as his modus operandi. What we need is to know as much about La Llorona as he does. That way we can be there before he makes his next move," Johnson declares. "Oh my God Ramirez, you're a Latino; you know exactly where to go to find out more about La Llorona," Johnson adds jokingly.

"Yes I do know where to go but you have to understand these people take their religion seriously. You cannot go in there making fun of them or go in there pushing people around, because if they can't put a hex on you they might cut us both up and use our body parts to decorate their temples; some of these people are crazy," Ramirez says.

"Come on now Ram I know you know somebody and I know how to act professionally in front of real witches," Johnson jokes.

"The fact is I do know somebody but he won't talk to us unless we agree to a cleansing," says Ramirez.

"Hey I'm always clean and well dressed, thank you," Johnson proclaims.

"He meant spiritual cleansing he's afraid one of us is in great danger," says Ramirez.

"Oh, My, God;…you mean La

Llorona is after us now?" Johnson jests. "We couldn't be that lucky you see; La Llorona is a minor demon or tortured soul tricked into doing a greater demon's bidding, and since she is his best soul collector, well you and I are kind of pissing him off by trying to stop her," Ramirez continues.

"That is why he wants us get a cleansing to make sure no other demon spies are there when he gives us the info we need on La Llorona."

"Okay I'll do it but, that does not mean I believe this mumbo jumbo," Johnson adds.

"Great, we're meeting him at his house tomorrow at seven so pick me up at the Spring Branch substation," says Ramirez.

"What time are you clear over there and where is his house?" Johnson asks.

"Anytime after four and his house is in Little Mexico, over by Wayside and Canal. So eat a light lunch; I know a great restaurant that is just five minutes from his house," Ramirez continues. "We can be over there eating an early dinner while the rest of Houston fights rush hour, FYI I'm buying."

"You know Ramirez, I just knew there was something good about this case," Johnson adds as here puts his coat on and walks away.

"Laterz!" Ramirez says as continues with his paper work at his desk.

The next day Johnson arrives at the sub station as Ramirez is cramming papers into his briefcase.

"You're early," says Ramirez.

"How can someone be early to a free dinner, plus we got to beat that rush hour traffic and it's already half past four you're late," Johnson explains.

Moments later both officers are in a car headed east on interstate ten, (aka the beast) as they pass the Memorial area, Ramirez notices a man standing on the railway overpass far ahead of them. He quickly yells at his partner when he realizes the man is holding a cinder block. "Look out!" he exclaims as he points at the man on the over pass. Johnson slams on his brakes and makes a hard right as the cinder block smashes into the car behind them. Johnson barely manages to control the car onto the grass embankment a few feet after the overpass. Ramirez exits the vehicle gun in hand almost before it stops, as he reaches the top of the railway overpass he yells. "Stop!" but the only thing on the overpass is one black crow that turns towards him and caws once then flies away. Johnson is close behind also with his gun drawn and halfway out of breath saying.

"Where'd he go?"

"I don't know," gasps Ramirez "I don't know."

Both officers quickly compose themselves and return to their car below, a couple of

HPD squad cars are on the scene and in control. Luckily no one was hurt seriously; the cinder block had gone though the other cars windshield and snapped the empty passenger's seat in half. Ramirez and Johnson give the officer in charge a brief statement as an ambulance arrives.

"Sorry I can't give you more but he was too far away and we were going too fast, he was a big guy at least six foot with long black hair, wearing a black straight rim cowboy hat, with black shirt, pants and coat, but his coat was different than most coats I've seen it was like half coat, half cape," Johnson describes.

"It was a duster one of those old time western horseman's coats," adds Ramirez

"My granddad had one."

"Well boys I won't hold you up any longer thanks for your help," says the officer as Johnson and Ramirez climb into their car.

"Wow look at the time it's six thirty we'd better go straight to our meeting," states Ramirez while looking at his watch.

"I thought you were buying dinner, I can't believe you're gonna use a little rock falling off a bridge as an excuse not to buy dinner!" Johnson exclaims.

"Don't worry dinners still on me but we'll just have to go after the meeting," Ramirez assures his partner.

A half hour later Ramirez finds himself hanging his head out the window of the vehicle trying to find the address of the

Curandero's house as Johnson complains

"Is it this one or are we lost just like my dinner."

"Hold on," says Ramirez "This one is eight thirty nine so the next one should be it, eight forty one that's it that's his house!" Both officers exit the vehicle and walk towards a small meager yet very well adorned house.

8 MODERN DAY MYSTIC

"Wow this is nice kind of reminds me of my Nana's house," says Johnson.

"I told you these are just people with a little different religion," Ramirez states.

"Don Pedrito! Don Pedrito!" calls out Ramirez.

"Aye voy aye voy," Don Pedrito answers.

"Soy yo sargento Ramirez," Ramirez says.

"I know who you are and welcome to

my humble home; come in, come in, can I offer you gentlemen something to drink? I have fresh tea or coffee and some Mexican cookies," Don Pedrito invites.

"Coffee and cookies sounds great to me, we had a small problem and I missed dinner," Johnson interjects.

"I know," says Don Pedrito. "That dark man with a big rock barely missed you but you are safe in my home." Johnson and Ramirez look at each other wondering how this small, feeble, old man could possibly know anything about what just happened to them miles away from here unless he could fly like a bird. Johnson thinks then shrugs his shoulders and says

"Well how about that coffee?"

"Follow me to the backyard. Coffee, tea and cookies are already on the table; help you while I and my assistants prepare ourselves for the ceremony."

After walking into the backyard Johnson and Ramirez sit down and enjoy fresh coffee and cookies. Moments later Don Pedrito and his five assistants enter the backyard wearing white robes. As Don Pedrito begins to explain, two of his assistants begin to draw two circles, one about thirty eight feet in diameter and one encompassing the first circle about forty feet in diameter on the ground with salt. The assistants are very focused on their task one begins the inner circle in a counter clockwise direction, the larger circle is begun in a clockwise rotation as they both meet on the completion of their circle they kneel making the sign of the crucifix on their torso and return to the side of Don Pedrito.

"The first circle holds things in, the second keeps thing out we use salt as a symbol of purity," Don Pedrito informs. A third assistant goes to the center of the circle lighting a pure white candle (which is about four feet tall and one foot in diameter) while he prays in a low tone.

Two other assistants begin to draw the symbol of a pentagram inside the inner circle. Don Pedrito explains, "The candle is a gift to the saints in exchange their for knowledge. While the pentagram is the symbol of the five elements earth, wind, fire, water and spirit." Upon completion of the pentagram all three assistants face each other making the sign of the crucifix upon their torso and return to Don Pedrito's side. Now that Don Pedrito and his assistants are all together standing in a circle, a large crucible with incense is lit, five smaller crucibles are filled from the large crucible. Don Pedrito takes the large crucible to the center of the pentagram where the crucible begins to emit a large billowing white cloud which seems to form a canopy over the entire yard. Simultaneously, his assistants have picked up their small crucibles by their hanging chain in their left hand and a bundle of herbs (various aromatic herbs grouped together about two feet long) in their right hand. They then approach Ramirez and Johnson walking around them several times while praying in some forgotten language while gently brushing the officers from head to toe with the herbs.

The scent of sandalwood, patchouli, frankincense, myrrh, peppermint, rosemary and sage seem to fill the air and energize the tired and weary officers. One by one the assistants proceed from their walk around the officers to a walk around the outer circle then for a walk on the inner circle each one stopping at his prospective point of the pentagram.

Don Pedrito waves at the officers to join him

at the center of the pentagram as he sits on the ground and invites them to do the same. Ramirez and Johnson comply as Johnson says

"Okay now what?"

"Now nothing; I just think it's really cool to do this so I could sit and think in the backyard," Don Pedrito remarks.

"Sorry I couldn't resist, I just like the look on people's faces when I say that," says the now spry, old Curandero.

Johnson smiles and hangs his head finally admitting defeat.

"All joking aside," continues Don Pedrito "You gentlemen have come here for answers but all I can provide for you is the purest form of the legend of La Llorona that was told to me by my grandfather he passed on to the next world at one hundred and nine years old another ten years and I'll tie his record, he told me this story when I was just a young boy and constantly reminded me to never forget the details because one day they might prove useful. So now I will tell the story to you; the cleansing was to make sure no evil had followed you here and the ceremony we have just performed will prevent all forms of evil from seeing or hearing what I have to say, for you see La Llorona is just a poor tortured soul that keeps being tricked into committing the same crime over and over again; she is no real danger to someone like myself; but the demon that controls her. Now he could be a real problem so let us deal with this young lady first she's not as hard to handle," says Don Pedrito.

9 MEXICAN MYSTERY

"I can remember my grandfather giving his personal accounts on this matter as if it were yesterday…" Don Pedrito continues waving his hands through the air as if he was drawing a picture. The light from the candle seems to grow brighter as bright as the sun and we find ourselves in an open field of tall grass in the early eighteen fifties and nearby is a wagon trail leading to a small town on the Rio Grande quite possibly what is nowadays Matamoros, Mexico. A lone caballero is riding down the dusty trail into town looking for work his first stop is the stables where he leaves his horse boarded. He inquires about a rancher hiring men to move cattle north.

"I heard there is a man hiring vaqueros to move cattle north," says Pedro.

"Yes a Gringo arrived about a week ago looking for Vaqueros but there is not as many men in this town as there used to be. He was hoping to find forty or fifty men in a day or two but people don't come here like they used to not since La Llorona started killing folks around this area," says the stable keep as he sighs sadly.

"Who is La Llorona and why is she killing people?" Pedro asks.

"Ask the bartender at the saloon he knows all about her and the Gringo, plus he can get you a very nice room cheap," responds the stable keep.

"Thanks," says Pedro as he takes his saddlebags off the horse and slings them over his shoulder then retrieves his Hawkens rifle.

"Take good care of Paco and give him some extra oats," he continues as he tosses a silver coin at the stable keep.

"I sure will, only the best for Senor Paco!" replies the stable keep with a smile on his face and a gleam in his eyes as Pedro walks away. Pedro finds the streets almost deserted as he walks towards the saloon. The town is quite large, most of the buildings look almost new and well built yet most of the businesses seem to have been abandoned. The people peeking out their windows might have found Don Pedrito's Granddad (Pedro) a strange sight to see. Everything he wore was tan; hat, boots, duster, and gun holsters even his Hawkens rifle had a tan strip of cloth wrapped around it.

Pedro is amazed to see the size of the Saloon; why, Paco could have fit through these doors. He notices a large colored poster announcing a show with dancing girls in pretty dresses and live music every Friday night, but the date on the poster is a year old. Once inside he finds the place spectacular from its polished granite floors to the gigantic crystal chandelier which hung high above a very large stage.

There were a few people enjoying drinks and playing cards but it was a little too quiet for a saloon so he walks up to the bar and inquires about a room for the night.

"What can we do you for?" asks the bartender as he polishes his bar with a rag.

"One beer and one room with a bath for the night," responds Pedro.

"One cervesa coming right up and that will be fifty cents for the room including two meals and twenty cents for the bath and your first beer is on the house," replies the bartender.

"The stable master said you knew where to find the Gringo hiring vaqueros to move cattle north," Pedro inquires as he receives his beer.

"Oh jes, the Gringo is the man wearing the boat captains cap playing cards at that table he's looking for men to move a herd north of here next week and he is offering double pay for the right kind of man," the bartender informs him.

"He also said you could tell me about some lady called La Llorona that's going around killing folks in the area," Pedro says as he notices that both eyes on the man he's speaking to are completely white.

"Come back later after you talk to the Gringo and I'll be glad to tell you all about her and my blindness," responds the bartender.

Pedro walks over to the card table and excuses himself for interrupting the gentlemen's card game.

"Begging your pardon for the interruption gentlemen, but I hear you are hiring vaqueros and I am in need of work."

"No pardons needed here young man, I am in great need of good vaqueros are you any good with that Hawkens?" asked the bearded man in the mariner's cap.

"Yes sir if you can see it I can hit it; hunting is very important to survival in this area," remarks Pedro.

"Good I'm moving five hundred head of cattle north and I need to keep them safe from wild animals, cattle rustlers and quite possibly Apaches," continues the Gringo.

"So if you're not scared of this La Llorona and you have a good horse consider yourself hired. I'll give you two dollars a day and three square meals daily. If you find this agreeable meet me at the stock yard tomorrow and I'll fill you in on more of the details, because I need to start moving these cattle across the Rio Grande no later than Monday morning," says the Gringo.

"Gracias Senor I'll be at the stock yard before first light," Pedro replies as he excuses himself.

He walks back to the bar where the bartender informs him his room and bath is ready.

"Here you go number six up the stairs third room on the right the water should be nice and hot if you like my cousin does laundry for ten cents a set. Just put your clothes in the bag on the bed and bring it to me. She will have it all clean and back to you by morning."

"Good I'll bring it down after my bath, con permisso," says Pedro as he heads to his room. Soon he is enjoying his bath relaxing in the hot water as he submerses his head under the water he is startled by a shadow that seems to pass over the tub and quickly jumps up cocked pistol in hand searching the entire room with his eyes taking small steps to insure he doesn't slip while standing in the tub he makes one complete turn and finds nothing, ghosts Pedro thinks to himself or just old memories. A woman's laughter in the adjacent room breaks his train of thought. So he puts his pistol down on a table next to the tub and continues with his bath. Moments later Pedro exits his room with a laundry bag slung over his shoulder. Once again he hears a light-hearted laughter coming from the room next door as he locks his door. He continues down the stairs to the bar where he sets his laundry bag on the counter and asks the bartender about dinner. "Here is my laundry and what time is dinner?"

"Dinner is on the way, I hope you like arroz con pollo," says the bartender.

"You can sit anywhere you like being that you're our only tenant this evening," continues the bartender. "As a matter of fact you're the first person to rent a room this week; the Gringo always stays at the Dela Garza hacienda. So that makes us the only two people in this whole place, business have really gone to shit," the bartender says with a sigh. "What about the girl in the room next to mine?" Pedro asks.

"You saw her?" exclaims the bartender.

"No but I heard her laughing she sounds quite happy why is something wrong?" Pedro replies.

"No, not if you didn't see her, that used to be Angelica's room, before she disappeared and took my business with her," says the bartender. "I believe she was La Llorona's first victim, even if her body was never found, I know that pinche brujo killed the star of my show," he cries as he wipes his eyes with his bar rag. "You know Angelica was a true star, she studied dance in Paris," he continues spinning the bar rag over his head.

"She taught the other girls a dance from there; why it was so provocative men came from hundreds of miles away just to see them dance," the bartender claims. "So?" Pedro asks. "What happens to her? Where are the other girls? Why do men avoid this town and who the hell is La Llorona?" Pedro continues. "Everyone seems to know her name but no one ever says very much about her as if they are afraid of her."

"Con permisso, one moment," says the bartender sniffing the odor of the food entering the saloon. "Maria aqui en la barra esta bien," the bartender directs the young lady towards the bar with the food. Then hands her some money and Pedro's laundry.

"Bien here is your food and I will try to explain what has happened to this town and who I think La Llorona is while we eat,"

"Bueno," Pedro agrees as he helps himself to the food.

"Look I know you're going to find this hard to believe, but just two years ago this saloon was a show place like no other. A young girl named Angelica had just arrived from Paris she convinced me to finance a dance show."

"She didn't have to do too much convincing once she showed me a few other things she had learned in Paris. She explained to me how the dance was like an advertisement for a courtesans physical talents," he said. "The dances were set to galope style music and the dancers would take the stage in line formations lifting their dresses and kicking so high you could see their underwear. After a few shows some Dons, Bankers and Wealthy Gringos would pay handsomely for the tables closest to the stage, each hoping to secure the dancers services for the night. Angelica not only demanded a high price she was also showered with gifts and marriage proposals but she was all business and her business was pleasure. Then one day she confided in me that she was pregnant with a child and she had no intention of becoming a mother. Angelica said this would ruin my business and her career; this child could not be allowed to destroy her beautiful body. She begged for my help," the bartender continued as he wept.

"It's my entire fault for her death, my blindness and the curse on this town. I am the one who told her where to find the Brujo's shack down by the river; she was never the same after her first visit to that pinche brujo's place. She became quiet and recluse, refusing to perform or see customers staying locked in her room. A few weeks later on a dark night I found her filling a bag with money ranting about seeing the brujo to get her ninio (child) back. I tried to stop her but she already had her horse waiting outside and myself being barefoot all I could do is watch as she and her horse disappeared into the fog."

"The next day when her horse returned to town without her. I assembled a group of twenty well-armed men and a priest to go confront El Brujo. We found his shack abandoned but his fireplace was still lit and many dead animals still dripping blood adorned his ceiling in one corner there was an altar of black onyx eight foot high with a winged skeleton standing in front of it. I had never seen a skeleton such as this, the skull was shaped like a snake. It had big twisted horns like a ram and hands twice the size of a mans with four inch claws, but strangest of all was that it seemed to have one human foot and one hoofed foot. The Priest claimed this place was full of evil magic and demanded it be burned down and the men quickly obeyed; as it burned some of the men became very ill and the rest were filled with fear so half of them returned to town. The rest of us separated into parties of two to search the river's edge for the Brujo and Angelica."

"Before we began our search the Priest gathered us together for a blessing and gave us each three silver bullets out of a wooden box he carried. He claimed these bullets were made and blessed by a Jesuit Priest and if we should encounter the Brujo we should not give him a chance to speak for he could bewitch us. Soon the sun began to set, somehow I lost sight of my partner, then I heard a woman cry; "Mi Ninio-,Mi Ninio-," it was Angelica's voice. I ran toward the sound of her voice, but all I found was the horror of a demon feasting on my partner," he said sadly.

"The light of my torch betrayed me, the demon turned towards me even as it continued to suck the life juices out of my partner as it held him in mid-air. I was paralyzed as it slowly retracted its' three foot tongue from my partners mouth and tossed his withered, worm infested corpse onto the rocks. I forgot all about my gun and magic bullets. I turned to run but I slipped on the wet rocks and hit my head. The next thing I remember was a doctor telling me I was blind, later the two men that had found me and brought me home informed me that we three had been the only survivors, even the ten men that left early never made it home. Their rotten corpses were found no more than a mile from town, both men gave me their magic bullets and left town never to be seen again. Since then many have seen the woman crying by the river looking for her child but they say if you come too close she is so hideous she will make you blind and turn your hair white."

"Look." the bartender continues. "I'm not saying they will work, but maybe if a man with true courage has these," the bartender states as he places nine silver bullets on the bar. “Yes, maybe then La Llorona can be sent back where she belongs and the curse on this town might be removed. I’m not asking you to hunt her down but you’ll be near the Rio Grande almost three days it’s possible she could come to you and without these you will be helpless,” the bartender informs him. “The bullets are on the house but if La Llorona crosses your path, do a poor blind man a favor and put one in the bitch’s heart for me.” Pedro considers the blind man’s wisdom then accepts the bullets but insists on paying for them.

“I’ll take the bullets but you must accept some payment for them, because I consider it bad luck to receive any weapon as a gift,”

"Good," the bartender replies. "That will be one cent," says the bartender while holding out his hand. Pedro pays him and both men finish their dinner, soon after Pedro returns to his room. The rest of the night is cool and quiet. Pedro is happy for a nice bed for daybreak will come early and driving cattle is hard work.

10 TEXAS LEGEND

The Gringo finds Pedro at stockyards as the sun begins to rise. “Good, you’re early. Do you know how to read a map?” says the gringo as he unrolls a map on a nearby table.

“Yes,” Pedro answers.

“Great we have to move these cattle twenty miles west; there is a shallow spot in the river right about here this time of the year. You should be able to reach that spot early enough to make camp there for the night, then cross the entire herd over the next day. You can head back east staying close to the river, letting the cattle graze and load up on water a couple of days then head north somewhere about here," says the Gringo as he points to different spots on the map. He then rolls up the map and hands it to Pedro and says with a smile.

"Congratulations you're the new trail boss; the last one never returned to the bunkhouse last night. You'll get a fifty dollar bonus if you get my cattle home."

"Thank you Senor I will not fail you Senor," says Pedro.

"Don't. I'm entrusting you with ten men, thirty boys and five hundred head of cattle; more than a ten percent loss of any of the three is not acceptable. You will find Cookie and Federico a great help to you in any situation. I'm taking my boat down river and cutting across the gulf up Baffin Bay, myself and some more men will meet you at Laureles in two weeks good luck and adios," says the Gringo as he shakes Pedro's hand then walks away.

Pedro has a quick chat with Federico and Cookie; before beginning their task of moving the herd. Cookie takes one man and two boys ahead to set up camp at their first stop on the river's edge. While Pedro, Federico and the rest of the group begin to move the herd west. The trip is relatively uneventful upon arrival the vaqueros smoothly secure the cattle and begin their rotation on watch as dinner is served. Once everyone has eaten Pedro assigns night watch, one man acting as the supervisor and ten boys rotating every four hours with the rest of the group. Each guard only a half a kilometer apart forming a half circle south of the river and using river to the north as a natural fence. This should keep the cattle in place for the night and allow everyone at least eight hours sleep. The night seemed to go smoothly except for one boy who is late reporting in from his watch the following morning. Pedro and the watch supervisor Federico ride out to find the boy.

They find the boy sitting on a large rock clenching the crucifix on his rosary. The boy seems unharmed but blind and incoherent;

below him near the rock is the dismembered carcass of his horse with its skull ripped in half at the jaw.

"La Llorona," says Federico as he makes the sign of the crucifix over his own torso.

"No it was probably a pack of coyotes!" exclaims Pedro.

"Even a hundred coyotes could not do this, look there is no blood!" Federico shouts.

"Look your boss is paying us good money to move these cattle, if the rest of the group hears about this they will quit and run home. Then how are we going to move these cattle a hundred and fifty miles my friend? This secret says between you and I; you will take the boy home, I will tell the others he was sick," Pedro explains as he help Federico put the boy on his horse. "Then you can cross the river at Matamoros and catch up to us," Pedro continues as Federico climbs on his mount. "Don't worry Federico I will keep a very good watch on everyone, I'll sleep on the chuck wagon a few hours a day and keep watch both nights while we are near the river. Now you get this boy home safely and stay away from the river at night, Now Go!" Pedro orders as Federico rides away.

Back at camp the vaqueros are ready to cross the river with the herd as Pedro arrives and explains that Federico had to take a boy home that was too sick to continue the drive. Most of the day is spent getting the herd across the river, but Pedro pushes hard towards the east trying to put some distance between them and whatever killed that horse. After dinner and Pedro's short nap, Cookie had some questions for Pedro.

“Is the boy alive?” asks Cookie.

“Of course he’s alive,” Pedro answers.

“Do you think it was her?” Cookie continues.

“No, it was just some hungry wild animals,” says Pedro.

"If she gets hungry again can you stop her?” Cookie interrogates further.

“That depends if she believes in these magic bullets as much as you believe in her," says Pedro as he loads the silver bullets into his .44 caliber Colt Navy revolvers. The rest of the night Pedro stays close to his trusted mount Paco because nothing can get past Paco's hearing not even when he's asleep.

Fortunately all was quiet the entire night, maybe she was full of horse meat or maybe they had outrun her for good, yes maybe. In the morning Pedro and the vaqueros pushed east, almost everyone seemed happy to reach their last camp by the river the next morning they would be able to head north and leave the river and her far behind them. Cookie had spoken to the older vaqueros and they agreed to partner up for each of the four hour watches that night. This way there would be two fully armed vaqueros keeping an eye on the boys in case of trouble and Pedro could rest before the journey north.

Now Cookie had really planned to make this evening special for all the men.

Not only had he prepared the finest brisket known to man, but he had put extra seasoned pork, garlic and cilantro into his melt in your mouth pinto beans and if that wasn't enough his peach cobbler with cinnamon would be.

Pedro slept like a rock there was nothing like a hard day's work followed by a delicious meal to put a man's mind at ease.

The night air was crisp and cool the stars seem close enough to touch and the sound of the Rio Grande flowing was all that was needed for a peaceful serenade of a vaquero's guitar and harmonica. This was truly a good night; suddenly the ground seemed to shake as gun fire erupts in the field near the river the bellowing of the cattle on the brink of stampeding fill the air with fear. It was sheer pandemonium the flash from the barrels of rifles seem like lightning cowboys and full grown vaqueros alike scream for their lives. Pedro had to fight his way through a crowd of young cowboys in disbelief of the horror that had just beset them just to reach Paco.

Fortunately Paco was always ready for a good fight, as soon as Pedro was in the saddle Paco quickly turned towards the gun fire and began his regal prance into the fray as his master readied his Hawkens rifle to fire. Pedro guided his mount towards the shouts of the vaqueros.

Luckily there is a full moon providing the vaqueros plenty of light to distinguish their target which seems to be half woman, half rotten corpse. When Pedro is close enough to see the demon he cannot get a clean shot off with his Hawkens because there is another vaquero and his horse between him and the beast. The demon seems to grow in size as the vaqueros' horse rears up to kick at her but the horse is no match for this demon as it quickly slaps the horses head clean off leaving a confused headless animal spewing blood out if its neck where his head used to be, stumbling in the dark and its rider in the claws of the beast. Pedro quickly capitalizes on this moment he draws a clean bead on the demon's head with his Hawkens rifle.

While Paco becomes stiff as a statue as if to aid his master in his shot. The blast from the Hawkens rifle echoes like the thunder in the night, but much to the disbelief of Pedro the beast merely turns towards him and acknowledges his presence. The demon's eyes seem to glow red as the embers in a fire.

She roars like a mountain lion as she tosses the vaquero in her claws towards him with one hand. Paco quickly moves to his right narrowly avoiding the screaming vaquero as he whizzes by and splatters like an over ripe melon on a large rock just behind them. Realizing his Hawkens rifle is of no use against the demon Pedro holsters his rifle. Knowing he needs to get much closer to use his revolvers he dismounts Paco and orders him to flee Paco reluctantly obeys. Shots ring out from the remaining vaqueros who are now coming to Pedro's aid the beast seems to be momentarily distracted by the barrage of bullets. This is all the advantage Pedro was hoping for as he runs towards the demon firing sequentially with each pistol. Three rounds from each of Pedro's colt navy revolvers strike with deadly accuracy at the demon's heart. The demon roars out, "Mi Ninio! Mi Ninio!" The center of its chest seems to ignite in flames as it thrashes its body on the ground then slowly claws its way back into the dark waters of the river gently crying, “Donde esta mi ninio?”

“This is when,” Don Pedrito says as he claps his hands once and we all seem to return to the old Curandero’s back yard, “My Grandfather realized that Angelica, the beautiful courtesan and La Llorona are one in the same,”

“Hold on just a second you did say: 'Are one and the same' not we're one in the same, why?” Johnson continues. “Didn’t you just tell us your Grand Papi killed her?”

“No I did not, I told you he used some of the magic bullets to send her back where she belongs but that is only temporary. You see she keeps being reborn and given another chance to correct her mistakes," says Don Pedrito.

"Unfortunately there is a greater evil that helps her commit the same mistakes over and over again, thus keeping her trapped here to do his bidding," Don Pedrito adds.

"So what you are saying is that if someone doesn't shoot her with some magical bullets she's just going to continue to go around killing people as she pleases?" asks Johnson.

"Oh-my-god! I think he's got it Ramirez," says Don Pedrito.

"Look this is impossible I don't believe in La Llorona or magic bullets," states Johnson

"That's ok Rupert; but your Grandmother, Alice said I should help you anyway," Don Pedrito responds. Johnson is speechless nobody knew his middle name much less his grandma's name.

"Ok let's say I believe a little of this; which I don't, where in the hell would I find magic bullets and where would I find La Llorona so I could shoot her?" Johnson asks.

"The first part is easy," Don Pedrito says as he displays three .44 caliber silver bullets in the palm of his hand each bearing the symbol of the crucifix.

"Oh my god, but those won't fit my gun," Johnson proclaims.

"You're in luck my Grandfather also left me this," Don Pedrito answers as he hands Johnson a mint condition Colt Navy revolver. “It has been kept in perfect firing order and the powder in the cartridges has been replaced by one of my assistants to insure their function. Now as for finding La Llorona I’m pretty sure even those that thought they had her under control are having problems finding her.”

“Wow now this is a beautiful work of art,” says Johnson as he admires the Colt Navy.

“Unfortunately it is against my beliefs to gift a weapon to anyone, I believe this would bring bad luck to the bearer of the weapon therefore I am obligated to sell this pistol to you,” remarks Don Pedrito.

“Now now hold on I don’t like it that

much a gun like this would cost more than I make all month," Johnson replies.

"Agreed then the weapon and bullets are yours for the grand total of one American penny," says Don Pedrito.

"Now you're talking," Johnson smiles as he digs in his pocket trying to find a penny.

"Hey Ramirez you got a penny I could borrow, I know you got a penny don't lie," Johnson adds.

Ramirez hands Johnson the penny shaking his head in disbelief as Johnson passes the penny onto Don Pedrito.

"It has been a pleasure doing business with you," Johnson says with a smile.

"Take good care of my Grandfather's

gun and it will take good care of you. Now if you want to find La Llorona there is a secret group in this city that believes they could hide their illegal pursuits from the law with ritualistic blood sacrifices. The light skinned man that you spoke to yesterday knows more about these people but it might take a little convincing to get him to spill the beans. You see this group practices black magic and likes to make examples of those who betray them. They are not only fearless and loyal to their leader they are also known to be completely ruthless and are not above human sacrifices," Don Pedrito informs the officers.

"It sounds like you know quite a bit about these people also can't you help us a little more?" Ramirez asks.

"No I am not as strong as I used to be when I was younger," Don Pedrito admits with a smile. "Now that I am old and tired I can only hope to shield their sight from what you now know and the weapon you possess," Don Pedrito continues. "If they knew what was happening here tonight they would concentrate all their efforts on destroying all three of us. Most of their members do have a tattoo somewhere on their body of a crown over two crossed Machetes this is all I could do for now."

"That is fine Don Pedrito we appreciate all your help I am sure you need your rest. I and officer Johnson need to get going home also, I can't believe there is still so much light out tonight," says Ramirez.

"That is because it is no longer night but morning young man," Don Pedrito states. Johnson and Ramirez look at their watches in disbelief. Both men are soon in the car waving out the window as the sun rises.

11 HOMECOMING

Johnson and Ramirez breathe a little easier once they are back on I-10 headed home. Ramirez dozes off almost immediately but it is not a restful sleep. It's more of a short series of nightmares and flashes of horrid images of a beautiful woman swimming in a river wearing a long yet very see through white dress but when she emerges from the water she is blood covered and skinless. Johnson finds it strange that the freeway is almost deserted, and then he remembers this is Sunday. He knows his mind must be extremely tired for several times on the way home he thinks he imagines the cowboy from the overpass standing on the side of the freeway staring at him as he drove by. Soon he is dropping Ramirez off at his car and on his way home for some much needed rest. While showering several times he seems to see a strange shadow pass overhead but quickly dismisses this to fatigue. Johnson makes himself a sandwich as he tries to towel his hair dry. A few bites from the sandwich and a cold soda and it's off to sleep, yes sleep.

Johnson awakes to the sound of his phone ringing when he answers its Ramirez saying,

"It's about time you answered this is

the fourth time I called."

"I'm up; what time is it?" Johnson mumbles.

"It's six pm, I'm on my way to your place I should be there in ten minutes," says Ramirez.

"Cool," Johnson answers as he stumbles to the bathroom tossing his phone on the bed. A few minutes later as he is putting on his shoes his doorbell rings. Still half asleep he walks through the living room and opens the door.

"What the fu--, happened here?" says Ramirez. Both men are shocked as they look around the blood drenched room. What seems to be the beheaded carcass of a skinless goat hangs from the ceiling fan. The poor beast fur cover, horned head has had its cranium hollowed out to be used as receptacle for a burning black candle is in the center of the coffee table while it's dripping tongue with a sixteen penny nail driven through it adorns the inside of Johnson door. The symbol of a crown over two crossed machetes is painted in blood on his wall.

"Aw! Hell! No! They don't know who they are fu--in with! I'll kill them all! This is my house I'll kill these mother Fu--er!" Johnson yells in anger. Ramirez manages to calm him down and then both officers begin to call people on their phones within minutes a small army of investigators are on site gathering information. After giving his statement Johnson gives his key to the O.I.C. and tells him to lock up when they're done.

"Hey Johnson why don't we go pay Mac a friendly visit," says Ramirez.

"You read my mind partner," responds Johnson as he puts his taser and a bottled water into his briefcase.

When they arrive at Pleasurz Johnson asks Ramirez for a favor.

"Hey Ram put this water in your pocket."

"Why can't you put it in your pocket? I'm not thirsty plus they serve drinks here," Ramirez answers.

"Look my pockets are full I've got my taser in one pocket and this big ass .44 in the other plus I don't want Mac to know we have it," he says.

"What's the big deal about bottled water?" Ramirez asks.

"You'll see," Johnson responds.

12 SHOCKING TESTIMONY

The bouncer quickly moves out of their way as they enter the club. There is a girl wearing only a G-String dancing very provocatively to the song Hells Bells. The officers pause for a moment to admire the view.

"I love this song, don't you," says Ramirez.

"I do now," answers Johnson.

"How are you guys doing can I offer you gentlemen a drink or a girl? Just ask and it's yours the one on stage is brand new just got her today from Cancun," brags Mac.

"No we'd just like to have a word with you in private if you don't mind," Johnson asks.

"Sure let's step into my office," says Mac.

He leads the Officers down a narrow hall to an expensively decorated office with large hand carved leather cushioned chairs, complete with a couch and a gold leafed desk.

"Now what's on your mind?" asks Mac.

"We need information about an organization that uses a crown over two crossed machetes as their symbol," Ramirez inquires. “We have reason to believe they are helping your girl Angel evade police questioning.”

“Sorry gentlemen I’m afraid I don’t know what you’re talking about, Angel quit months ago she wanted to get an abortion to save her figure,” Mac answers.

“Why didn’t you mention that before what are you really hiding?” Ramirez asks as he grabs Mac by his jackets collar and slams him backwards on his fancy desk.

“Look you big stupid Mexican, you don’t know who these people are they will kill me if I say anything they don’t give a damn about the law, they will kill you too,” Mac shouts. Johnson grabs Ramirez by one arm and puts one hand on his back and says.

"Hold on Ram you can't just go knocking people's head around expecting them to give you answers they don't have. Can't you see this man is scared? Those Machete people must be very dangerous let the man go and let's talk about this like civilized human beings. If this man says they are ruthless killers there is no reason for us to doubt him after all we are police officers and should conduct ourselves in a professional manner," Johnson explains calmly.

"Now Mac I understand you're afraid of these people but what you need to understand is you should really be afraid of me; Motherfu--er!" Johnson exclaims as he steps back and fires his taser directly into

Mac's chest. Mac's body bounces off of his desk and onto the floor as he is electrocuted by the taser his body is still quivering from the jolt as Johnson proceeds to kick the man in his genitals.

"Now Mac let's talk about this like civilized human beings," continues Johnson as he signals Ramirez to give him the bottled water. "Every time I ask a question and you do not give me the answer I want," Johnson continues as he begins to pour the water on Mac. "I squeeze the trigger on this taser but do understand this is not your standard police issued taser, this is a ten million volt super taser not to mention you being all wet is gonna fry you like bacon in a pan. You see there's one thing I learned in my five years working vice all you perverts that run these gentleman's clubs like to have your offices sound proofed," Johnson proceeds. "Do you know what that means?" says Johnson as he helps Mac into a chair with a taser wires still connected to his chest. "That means that no matter how much noise we make or in this case you make as your skin begins to fry like so much chicken on the grill; nobody else will hear you scream. Now who in the hell are these Machete motherfu--ers?"

"I I don-," Mac tries to answer as ten thousand volts hit his wet body and smoke comes out of his hair.

"Wrong answer, now do you understand the rules of this game? A simple yes or no answer will do." says Johnson as he establishes his dominance of this situation.

"Yes," answers Mac as his body still quivers from the last shock it has received.

"Now same question who are these Machete people?" Johnson asks.

"They are a drug cartel out of southern Mexico with strong political connections in this city," Mac responds.

"Ok, now for the next question, where can I find these people?" says Johnson.

"They are all over this city man some of them are even cops you will nev---aaaahhh!!!!" Mac screams as lightning dances over his entire body once more.

"Wrong answer! I want an address and the next time you answer incorrectly; I'm going to squeeze this trigger till the battery runs out!" Johnson growls then composes himself. "Now where can I find these people?" he adds.

"I have an address for their main safe house in the top drawer of my desk it's written on the last page in a little blue book it's the only address on that page," Mac answers while uncontrollable tremors still pulse through his body."

"Now that wasn't so hard was it," says Johnson softly as he rips the taser needles from Mac's chest. He then proceeds to take the man's cell phone and keys out of his pockets and destroys the phone on his desk. “Don’t bother getting up we’ll lock all four of those locks on your door on our way out,” Johnson jests as he jingle the keys in front of Mac’s face. Ramirez and Johnson compose themselves as they lock all four locks (two of them double sided dead bolts) on the door. They smile and wave at the working girls as they leave the club.

13 DEATH'S DOOR

After driving back to the station Ramirez asks,

"How long do you think we have before they figure it out?"

"They'll get suspicious about closing time but they won't break the door down till five or six in the morning." answers Johnson. "That gives us about seven hours to hit these guys before anyone warns them. I know this area there is nothing but millionaire's mansions that have ten or more bedrooms with yards as big as an acre or two and these cartel guys probably got some heavily armed guards," Johnson continues. "So you go get your boys and swat and I'll get my guys and ask Captain Harvey if he can lend us a hand then we can all meet at this school parking lot," says Johnson as he points to a spot on a wall map. "That's just one mile down the road by two in the morning, you got it."

"Got it," Ramirez responds as he looks at his large multi-function watch and sets his timer.

"How or why would a man wear a watch that size? I could never wear one that big," Johnson comments as Ramirez walks away smiling and shaking his head.

A few hours later in an abandoned school parking lot a scout gives his assessment of the property they are about to raid.

"What you got Stevens?" barks out his C.O.

"We got two entries one at the front with an iron gate and two guards with side arms possibly nine millimeters," Stevens reports. "There is another entrance at the rear on a narrow walkway from the bayou they have two men there sitting on a bench one with a shotgun one with an AK-74 as far as in the house," Stevens continues. "We don't know the windows are painted black but what's really strange is none of the men we've observed has moved a muscle in ten minutes and FYI the whole place smell worse than a sewer."

"Ok gentlemen everyone has their assignments the power will be cut to the property in fifteen minutes," says the C.O. "You will have two minutes to get in position then it will be flash bang and you move in and we'll go to total daylight two minutes after that; any questions," the C.O. continues. "Let's ROCK."

The group of about thirty officers disperses from the parking lot to converge on the house. Ramirez and Johnson are taking the walkway from the bayou with two swat officers. Everyone is in place suddenly the lights go out on the property the two minutes seem to last for an hour even the air seems to sit still the night is so quiet Johnson can hear his own heartbeat.

Suddenly thunder and lightning explodes from within the house as men appear like a swarm of bees descending on their hive. The iron gates fly open like a sheet left on a clothes line during a storm. The flash from concussion grenades and gunfire create a strobe like effect on images of blood and guts that seem to feed the frenzy of panic and fear. With every image another flash with every flash another image of human suffering and demons from the darkest recesses of their minds.

Chaos and confusion rule the night and at the end of two minutes the light brings little comfort because the images are all too real in total light. The truth of the matter is that except for them, every living creature human or not in this house is dead. Yes an eternity of defending themselves against things no longer alive in two short minutes. The strike force had performed its task with precision down to the very second. The only thing that was not calculated into the plan of this raid was the sheer unadulterated evil of their opponent. Time is no longer relevant to this group, they stand in awe of the carnage before them; motionless, speechless and some thoughtless. Neither man nor beast has escaped the wrath of hell in this horrid chamber of death. A few officers lay in pools of blood where they slipped and fell. Others stand bathed in the blood that drips from the corpses hung from the ceiling and staircases. Some of the officers hung their heads in shame knowing they had actually fired on some of the poor creatures. In the center of what must be the main room of this castle like estate is an obelisk at least twenty foot tall made of onyx with the skeletal remains of an eight foot winged creature with horns and a crown.

It takes almost ten minutes for most of the men, including Johnson and Ramirez to regain their bearings. As most of the men realize reality a few lose their sanity; one glassy eyed officer is led by another out of the house as the man sings (Jimmy crack corn and I don't care) over and over again. A few other exits the building weeping uncontrollably either dragging or just plain leaving their weapons behind them. The C.O. and most of his senior officers regain control of the situation. Johnson and Ramirez continue to explore the rest of the house in hopes of finding more clues as to what has occurred here. In a large room located to the right of the main entrance sit's a man in a large gold leaf chair fit for a king.

The massive Victorian high back chair is adorned at the top of its crest with a single letter M made of pure gold.
Upon this golden throne still sit's a man probably in his late fifties or early sixties holding an unfinished drink in one hand and a half smoked Cuban cigar in the other. His

gray mustache and beard give a small clue to his age unfortunately half of his head from the nose up seems to have been bitten off by a very large creature of some sort is all Johnson can conclude as Ramirez comments

"I just hope whatever the hell did that is no longer around."

"Me too," Johnson replies. "But, take a look at this," he continues as he points out a small safe, "Let's get one of the boys to open this thing up; I wanna see what's in it." Ramirez requests a safe cracker on his radio and within minutes a man with a heavy duty drill and a large tool bag rips open the safe. Johnson carefully removes a glass gallon jar from within the safe. Tears roll down his cheeks as anger fills his eyes for inside the jar is an unborn almost fully developed fetus with its umbilical cord still attached.

Without a word he places the jar on the ground wrapping it in his own jacket and cries.

Ramirez radios for someone from the coroner's department to come retrieve the jar. Both officers compose themselves and agree it's time to leave this place.

14 PREMONITION

It is early morning as Ramirez and Johnson leave the mansion in separate cars. With all the problems that had occurred in recent days Johnson decides that he is better off getting a room in a really nice hotel. Maybe a change of scenery will help ease his mind from recent events. Once he is in a nice hotel room he can't help but remember that three separate clocks within the mansion that they had raided were all stopped as if frozen in time at one minute past midnight. He wondered if Ramirez had noticed the same thing, no matter a quick nap should clear things up.

Later that evening when Johnson awakens he remembers dreaming about a beautiful woman in a white dress swimming in a moonlit river; for some strange reason every time he would get close enough to see her clearly the vision of a clock stopped at one minute past midnight would appear.

Johnson dismisses the dream as a possible sign of hunger and decides to visit a nearby hamburger joint. While enjoying his dinner he tries to contact Ramirez several times with no success. After dinner on his way back to the hotel he notices the clock on the dashboard of his car is flashing twelve-o-one. He immediately attempts to call Ramirez again with no luck only a message stating he's not available ("This is Sergeant Ramirez, I am not able to receive your call at this time, if you would please leave a message I will get back to you as soon as possible.") at this time.

The clocks in the mansion, the clocks in his dream and now the clock in his car; well that's just too many coincidences.

After driving back to his hotel he sees that the actual time is only ten minutes past eleven. He decides to return to the mansion alone if necessary because he has a strong gut feeling that she (La Llorona) will be there again at one minute past midnight.

The detective arrives at the front gate of the mansion at eleven forty-five. He finds the gate chained and locked with police crime scene tape forbidding entrance. The officer exits his vehicle and proceeds to enter on foot squeezing between the gates under the chain. He no longer feels the need to enter the house instead chooses to take a walkway around it straight to the pathway behind it that leads to the bayou.

15 JUDAS KISS

As he nears the bench where the cartel guards were seated the night before, he notices something in the moonlit waters of the bayou. He attempts to walk quietly as he approaches the edge of the bayou, there in the water he sees a raven-haired beauty wearing a long yet very revealing white dress her hair seems to float in the water like fine woven silk in a gentle breeze. Somehow he can feel that she knows he's watching her. She turns towards him floating on her back displaying her ample bosom. Johnson is mesmerized by her sheer beauty her emerald green eyes sparkle in the moonlight like stars on a very clear night. For a moment Johnson forgets why he is here, the rest of the world no longer matters. All hopes, fears, troubles and worries seem to disappear as smoke rising to an endless sky. She seems to smile at him and begins to swim towards the edge of the water. Once near the shore she slowly begins to stand as the water flows from her silky hair and glistening on her magnificent form Johnson cannot help but imagine the taste of her ruby red lips. When her waist emerges from the water it is evident that she wears her sheer white dress and nothing more. Suddenly the ringing of his cell phone destroys the silence of the night and the patience of his host. Snakes suddenly seem to grow from her hair her emerald green eyes turn to smoldering red embers.

Then her ruby red lips turn to ravenous jaws as she opens her mouth wide like a snake and roars. Johnson stumbles backwards narrowly avoiding her claws and a green mist that spews from her mouth rolling to one side he quickly retrieves the .44 Colt Navy revolver from his waistband.

He struggles to regain his footing as he fires one shot at the beast that bounces off a rock near her. Johnson is astonished as a beast seems to freeze in her tracks she seems to stare directly at the weapon he now possesses it is almost as if she recognizes the old Colt from a previous encounter. Johnson no longer shaken holds the pistol with both hands even as he trembles with fear he is positive he can land the next round in her heart. The beast slowly retreats waist deep into the bayou the snakes in her hair transform back into lovely, raven locks. Her flaming eyes return to limped emerald pools of tears. Her ravenous jaws return to quivering lips as she cries "Mi ninio donde esta mi ninio."

Johnson's fears turn into compassion, this beast at one time must have been much like any other person. Capable of love and all too prone to human error and the guilt it can create. He remembers why he has come; one shot not in anger; one shot full of compassion; one shot to give a lost soul rest. Johnson steadies his hand draws a clean bead on her heart.

Suddenly a shot rings out Johnson looks down at his gun he is positive he did not fire a shot. He feels something warm and moist on his back as he reaches with his left hand and touches his back he feels a warm sticky liquid as he brings his hand forward he realizes it is his blood. Slowly he turns and sees his partner Ramirez his knees give way as he falls into his partner's arms. Ramirez helps him to the bench nearby as he takes the revolver from Johnson's hands his dying partner clutches at his watch which breaks and falls to the ground revealing a small tattoo of a crown over two Machetes. Johnson looks at Ramirez in disbelief and asks one question.

"Why?"

"Please try to understand I never wanted it to come to this but I had no choice," Ramirez responds.

"Why?" Johnson repeats.

"I could not let you or anyone else destroy a legend that has been part of our culture for over a thousand years,"

"How could you?" Asks Johnson as he struggles to breathe.

"Remember old friend the greatest trick the Devil ever performed; was convincing everyone he doesn't even exist," says Ramirez as he closes Johnson's eyes with his right hand.

"Now sleep old friend sleep." One last breath and Johnson sleeps. Ramirez stands with the Colt Navy revolver firm in hand as he looks at La Llorona near the edge of the water and says to her

"Aye Angelica! You! Will! Never! Learn! Hahahahaha…!" says Ramirez as he turns and slowly limps away into the darkness.

FIN

ABOUT THE AUTHOR

Edwin C. De La Rosa orphaned before age four, native Texan and world traveler. Previously known for writing short comedic scripts and later more serious plays such as "La Fuente Vive," "El Adventudero," "Amarilla," and "La Trajedia Angeles y Banditos." Attributes most of his writing skills to Mr. Jeff Baldwin, Greg Taylor and thousands of others at the Texas Renaissance Festival.

P.S. Edwin works as an Automotive Mechanic to support himself and his family while refusing to give up his dreams and aspirations of one day becoming a well-known author.

78620775R00096

Made in the USA
Columbia, SC
18 October 2017